W9-BPM-624

GUESS WHAT?

Written by **Mem Fox**

Illustrated by **Vivienne Goodman**

Voyager Books
Harcourt Brace & Company
San Diego   New York   London

First published 1988 by Omnibus Books

Text copyright © Mem Fox 1988
Illustrations copyright © Vivienne Goodman 1988

All rights reserved. No part of this publication may be
reproduced or transmitted in any form or by any means,
electronic or mechanical, including photocopy, recording,
or any information storage and retrieval system, without
permission in writing from the publisher.

Requests for permission to make copies of any part
of the work should be mailed to:
Permissions Department,
Harcourt Brace & Company, 6277 Sea Harbor Drive,
Orlando, Florida, 32887–6777.

Library of Congress Cataloging-in-Publication Data
Fox, Mem, 1946–
Guess what?/Mem Fox and Vivienne Goodman.
p. cm.
Summary: Through a series of questions to which the
reader must answer yes or no, the personality and occu-
pation of a lady called Daisy O'Grady are revealed.
ISBN 0-15-200452-1
ISBN 0-15-200769-5 (pbk.)
[1. Identify–Fiction. 2. Questions and answers–Fiction.]
I. Goodman, Vivienne, ill. II. Title.
PZ7.F8373Gu 1990
[E]–dc20 90-4127

The paintings in this book were executed in gouache
on watercolor paper. The originals are the same size as
the reproductions you see here.
The text type was set in Caxton Book
by Central Graphics, San Diego, California.
Printed and bound by Tien Wah Press, Singapore
This book was printed with soya-based inks on
Leykam recycled paper, which contains more than
20 percent postconsumer waste and has a total
recycled content of at least 50 percent.
Production supervision by Warren Wallerstein
and Ginger Boyer
Text design by Lydia D'moch

First Voyager Books edition 1995

Printed in Singapore

DEFGH
ABCDE (pbk.)

To Miss Nancy and Wilfrid Gordon
McDonald Partridge
—M. F.

To Tom and Sarah
—V. G.

Far away from here lives
a crazy lady called
Daisy O'Grady.

Is she tall?

Guess!

Yes!

Is she thin?

Guess!

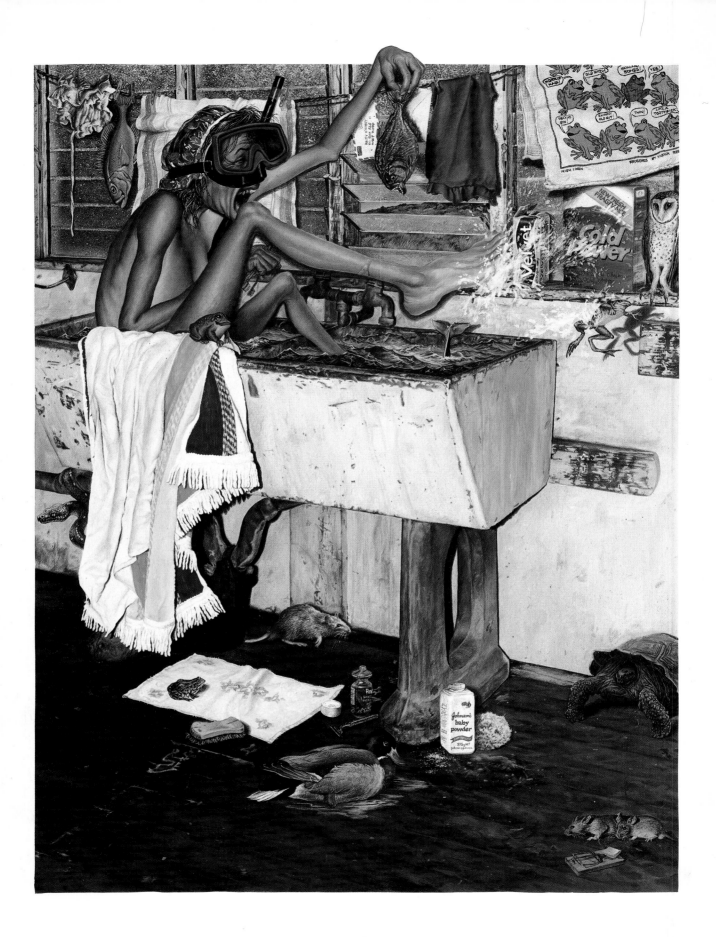

Yes!

Does she wear a long black dress?

Guess!

Yes!

Is she fond of animals?

Guess!

Yes!

Has she got a cat that's really
sleek and black?

Guess!

Yes!

Does she sometimes wear a hat?

Guess!

Yes!

Is it as black as her dress and her cat?

Guess!

Yes!

Does she like cooking?

Guess!

Yes!

Does she mix rats' tails, toenails,
and dead lizards' scales?

Guess!

Yes!

Does she have a broomstick?

Guess!

Yes!

Does she like to fly at night?

Guess!

Yes!

Is she a cursing, cackling,
cranky old witch?

Guess!

Yes!

Some people say she's really mean.

But guess what?

She's NOT!